Saltwater Crocodiles

by Grace Hansen

Abdo Kids Jumbo is an Imprint of Abdo Kids
abdopublishing.com

abdopublishing.com

Published by Abdo Kids, a division of ABDO, P.O. Box 398166, Minneapolis, Minnesota 55439.
Copyright © 2019 by Abdo Consulting Group, Inc. International copyrights reserved in all countries.
No part of this book may be reproduced in any form without written permission from the publisher.
Abdo Kids Jumbo™ is a trademark and logo of Abdo Kids.

052018

092018

THIS BOOK CONTAINS
RECYCLED MATERIALS

Photo Credits: Alamy, Getty Images, iStock, Minden Pictures, Shutterstock
Production Contributors: Teddy Borth, Jennie Forsberg, Grace Hansen
Design Contributors: Dorothy Toth, Laura Mitchell

Library of Congress Control Number: 2017960567
Publisher's Cataloging-in-Publication Data

Names: Hansen, Grace, author.
Title: Saltwater crocodiles / by Grace Hansen.
Description: Minneapolis, Minnesota : Abdo Kids, 2019. | Series: Super species |
    Includes glossary, index and online resources (page 24).
Identifiers: ISBN 9781532108259 (lib.bdg.) | ISBN 9781532109232 (ebook) |
    ISBN 9781532109720 (Read-to-me ebook)
Subjects: LCSH: Saltwater crocodile--Juvenile literature. | Body size--Juvenile literature. |
    Animals--Size--Juvenile literature. | Animal behavior--Juvenile literature.
Classification: DDC 597.982--dc23

Table of Contents

Giant Reptiles

Saltwater crocodiles are the

biggest **reptiles** in the world!

They can be found in parts
of Australia, India, and
Southeast Asia. They live
in both fresh and salt water.

They can weigh 2,200 pounds

(998 kg). That's more than

four American alligators!

saltwater crocodile

American alligator

9

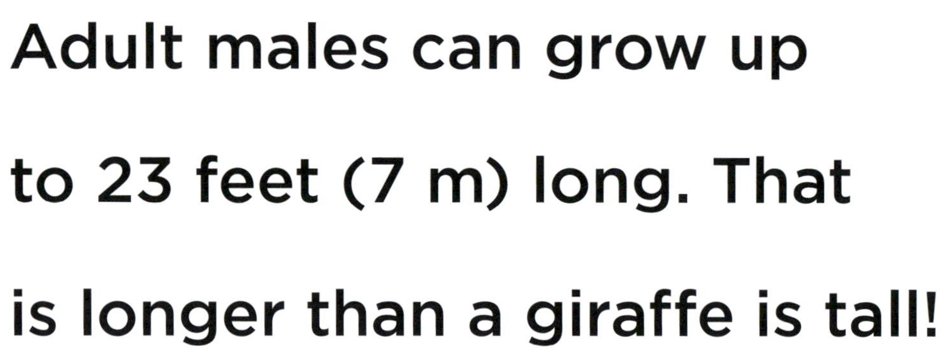

Adult males can grow up to 23 feet (7 m) long. That is longer than a giraffe is tall!

A saltwater crocodile's tail is long and strong. Its tail helps it move up to 18 miles an hour (29 km/h) in the water!

Saltwater crocodiles have the most powerful **jaws** in the world. Their big mouths have up to 68 teeth.

Hunting

They use their legs and tails to leap out of the water. They grab **prey** near the water's edge with their **jaws**.

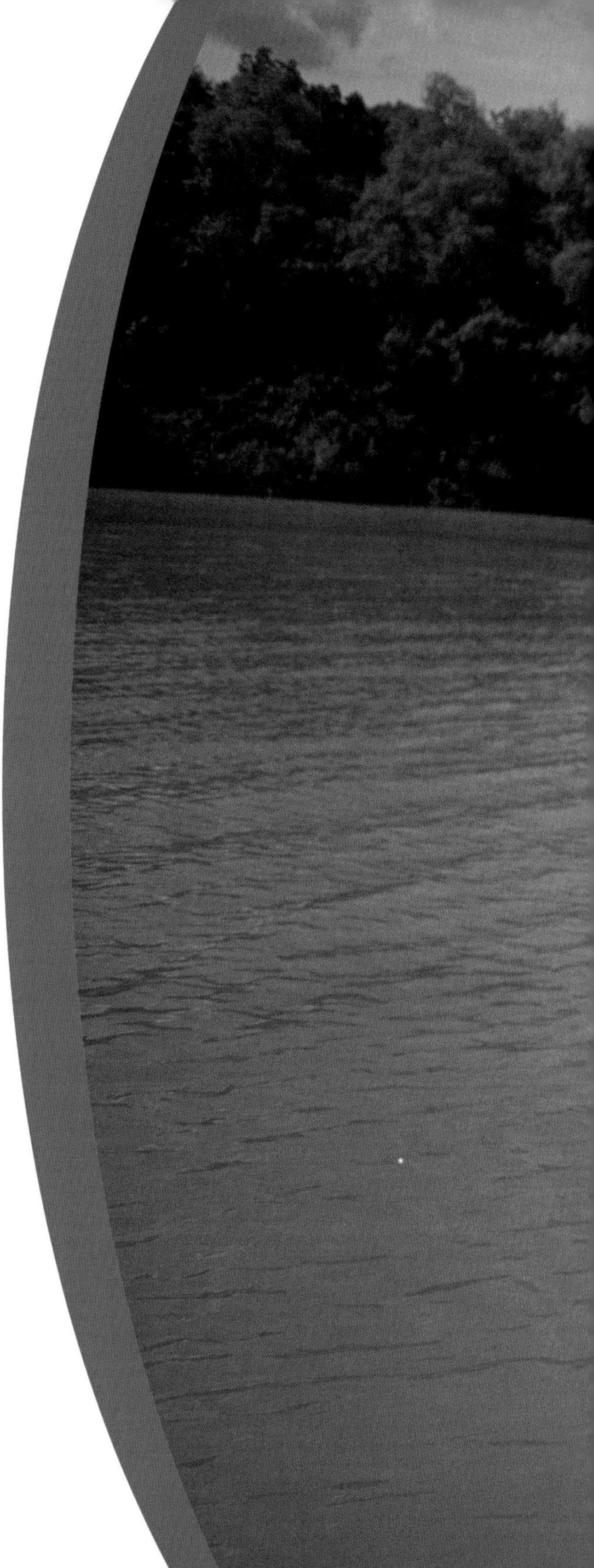

Babies

Female crocodiles make

nests. They lay up to 90 eggs.

18

Hatchlings are around 11 inches (27.9 cm) long. They are carried to the water in their mother's mouth. They may live up to 100 years!

More Facts

- Saltwater crocodiles will eat almost anything they can grab.

- Saltwater crocodiles are slower on land than they are in water. But they can reach speeds of more than 8 miles an hour (12.9 km/h) for a short time.

- Baby saltwater crocodiles have light yellow skin and black markings. As they age, they get much darker and have fewer markings.

Glossary

hatchling – a young animal that has just hatched from its egg.

jaws – the mouth parts of an animal that open and close for holding or crushing something between them.

prey – an animal that is hunted by another animal for food.

reptile – a cold-blooded animal with a skeleton inside its body and scales or hard plates on its skin.

Index

Visit **abdokids.com** and use this code to access crafts, games, videos, and more!